Glitched!

Written by **Jenny Jinks**

Illustrated by
Francesca Ficorilli

Chapter 1

"**Goal!**" Jenna cried.

"No fair. Offside!" Mattie and Aussie, Jenna's friends, cried out in unison. They were twin brothers.

Jenna did a victory lap around the pitch.

"Jenna, time to come off the computer now," Jenna's mum called. "Dinner time."

Jenna ignored her mum and carried on playing. She fiercely hammered the buttons and soon she was on the ball again, running back towards the goal. She was just about to score when...

"**JENNA!**" Mum shouted.

Jenna sighed. "Sorry, I have to go. I'll see if I can sneak back on later," she told her friends.

"And tell your friends you will *not* be back on later," her mum said through the door.

Drat!

Jenna switched off the computer and went downstairs for tea.

"You need to spend less time glued to that machine," Mum said over dinner.

"I'm just playing football with my friends," Jenna said. "You keep saying you want me to get into sports."

"I meant real sports, not a computer game," Mum huffed.

Jenna sighed. Why did her mum have to be so annoying? Playing computer games was fun. It took lots more skill to master a game on the computer than in real life. There were so many controls to remember! *And* there was far less risk of getting hurt. As far as Jenna was concerned, it was a win-win. Why didn't grown-ups get it?

Chapter 2

When Jenna got home from school the next day, she was in for a big surprise. For a moment, Jenna wondered if her mum had been abducted by aliens. There was a huge pile of dishes abandoned in the sink, and a mound of untouched ironing, but no sign of Mum. This was very unusual.

Jenna went upstairs to go on the computer, and there was Mum, playing a computer game!

"What are you doing?" Jenna asked in disbelief.

Mum didn't respond, she was too busy hammering on the keyboard. Gosh, that really was annoying. "MUM!"

"Oh sorry, I didn't hear you," Mum said, distracted.

"I've been playing this new game. It's called *Glitch*. Have you tried it? It's amazing."

"I've never heard of it," Jenna said, frowning. Mum didn't even look away from the screen once. What was going on? Mum never ever played computer games. And she wasn't even any good! Jenna watched her mum try to duck and jump across the land. She was rubbish!

Jenna just hoped she would come off soon.

But Jenna could not have been more wrong. Mum didn't stop to make dinner. Jenna had to make herself a sandwich. And when it was bedtime, Mum was still there, tapping away at the computer game. She barely even noticed when Jenna came to say goodnight.

When Jenna got up the next morning, she couldn't believe her mum was still there, staring at the screen.

"Have you even been to bed?" Jenna asked. Mum didn't look up. It was like she hadn't even heard her. And she looked terrible. The game had turned her into a zombie. She was obsessed. This was a disaster.

Jenna needed to make a plan, work out what to do. She needed the help of some gaming experts. She needed Mattie and Aussie.

Chapter 3

"You're never going to believe this," Jenna said when she met her friends at the park.

"Let me guess, your mum's become obsessed with a computer game?" Aussie asked.

"Yes!" Jenna cried. "Some weird new game called *Glitch*. How did you know?"

"Our parents are too," Mattie said. "They were on it all day yesterday."

"And all night," Aussie yawned.

"I don't believe it!" Jenna said. "What is this game doing to our parents?"

"It's like it's got them brainwashed," Mattie said.

"Well, we need to break the spell. We need to take the computers back!" Jenna said. The boys agreed.

As soon as they got home, they were going to take action. They would unplug the computers and rescue their parents from the evil brainwashing computer game... And then maybe have a go at it themselves!

Armed with a plan, Jenna went home. The post was still on the doormat and Mum clearly still hadn't done any cleaning. Jenna's dish was still on the table exactly where she had left it after breakfast. Mum must still be on the game.

But, when Jenna went upstairs to the computer, there was no Mum. Jenna's stomach did a flip. Something wasn't right. Where had Mum gone?

"Mum!" she called, as she searched the house, but her mum definitely wasn't home.

Jenna phoned Mattie and Aussie.

"Our parents are finally off the game!" Mattie said as soon as he answered the phone.

"Mum and Dad must have decided to go out. The computer is finally free," Aussie said.

"Your parents aren't there?" Jenna asked. "Weird. My mum's gone too."

The funny feeling in her tummy grew even bigger. She looked out of the window. The car was still there. Everywhere was quiet. A little too quiet. "I wonder where they've all gone."

"Who cares?" said Aussie. "Let's try out this new game and see what all the fuss is about!"

Jenna sat down at the computer and put on the headset. The name 'GLITCH' flickered on the screen, and a little character was running about at the bottom, ready to play. The character looked oddly familiar.

"Ready?" Aussie asked as two more characters popped up on the screen when Aussie and Mattie joined her in the game. They looked familiar too.

"I guess," said Jenna. But just as she was about to hit 'play', she froze.

No way. It couldn't be. Was that...

"WAIT!" she shouted.

"What? What's wrong?" Mattie asked.

One of the characters was waving madly at her. And Jenna realised immediately why it looked so familiar. It was...

"Mum!" Jenna cried. "My mum's in the computer game!"

Chapter 4

"No way," said Aussie.

"Wait, that's our mum and dad too!" Mattie suddenly cried. "What are they doing in there?"

"I think…" Jenna said hesitantly. "I think they've been taken into the game. They've been glitched!"

"This is mental. How has this happened?" Aussie asked.

"I don't know, but I don't think it's just our parents either. Haven't you noticed? The whole street is weirdly quiet, there's nobody about. I haven't seen any grown-ups for ages. Have you?"

"This is so weird," said Mattie, as they watched their parents waving their arms around and banging on the screen like they were trying to get out. "We have to find a way to get them out."

"Someone must have done this to them. We have to find out who made the game. Then we can find out how to rescue them," Jenna replied.

She did a quick search on the internet, but it was really hard to find anything. It was like the game didn't exist, as if it had just sprung up out of nowhere. Finally, she found some information.

"You won't believe it," she said. "The game is registered here, in our town. Let's go. We need to find out what they're up to!"

Jenna quickly scribbled down the address, and the three friends agreed to meet on the green before tracking down the culprit.

Chapter 5

They stared up at the address that Jenna had found. It was just an ordinary-looking house on an ordinary-looking street. Jenna knocked on the door and they waited for someone to answer.

"What if they're dangerous?" Mattie said.

"What if they're an evil genius?" Aussie went on.

"What if they're..."

"A kid!" Jenna said, as a boy not much younger than them answered the door. "Hi, are your parents home?"

The boy shook his head. Jenna felt bad for him, home all alone. Maybe his parents had been taken too.

"We think we know where they are. Can we come in?" Jenna asked.

The boy stared at the three of them, and then started closing the door.

Jenna put her hand out to stop him.

"Wait, please!" Jenna said. "I know this is going to sound crazy, but our parents have been taken into a computer game. We think your mum or dad might have made that game, and have accidentally glitched all the grown-ups in town and trapped them. We just want to help to get them back."

"I don't want them back," the boy said.

"What?" Aussie said, confused. "What do you mean?"

"All they do is try to spoil my fun: 'Not now, Graham.' 'You can't do that, Graham'," the boy said. "Well now they're gone and I can do whatever I like."

Jenna gasped. It wasn't an accident at all.

"It was you!"

Chapter 6

"Yes, it was me," Graham said proudly. "I made that game. I made it brainwash grown-ups so they couldn't escape it. And then I added a special glitch that sucked them into it completely. Now they're all trapped forever!"

"No!" cried Jenna. "There has to be a way out!"

"The only way out is the same for any game. They have to win," Graham said.

"So if they complete the game they get released?" Jenna asked.

"Well, yes," said Graham. "But let's face it, that's never going to happen. Grown-ups are useless, they'll never beat me. We're all better off without them, you'll see."

Then Graham shut the door in their faces.

Jenna stared round at her friends.

"What are we going to do now? It's one thing facing an evil genius, but a kid evil genius? We're doomed," Aussie said.

"Wait," Jenna said, beginning to smile. "I think I know how we can free our parents. Didn't you hear what Graham said? They just have to complete the game and they'll be saved."

"Yeah, but he's right—they're rubbish at computer games. It's never going to happen," Mattie said.

"Not on their own, maybe," Jenna said. "But there's one thing Graham has forgotten. They wouldn't be playing on their own now they are inside the game, would they? They need someone to play the game for them."

Jenna waited for a moment for the boys to work out what she was saying, but they stared at her blankly.

"Us!" Jenna cried. "We'll be the ones playing the game! If we can just control them and get them through to the end, then they'll be free. And if there's one thing we're good at, it's computer games!"

Mattie and Aussie grinned.

"Now let's go and get our parents back!"

Chapter 7

"Ready?" Jenna said into the phone as the three friends sat down at their computers, their parents jumping around on the screen in front of them, desperate to escape.

"Ready," Mattie and Aussie replied.

"Mum, if you can hear me, just do what I tell you. We're going to get you out," Jenna said.

Then the three friends hit the start button, and the game began.

Their parents appeared on a path in a forest. Jenna hit the button and her mum started running forwards. Jenna quickly got to grips with the controls and was soon telling her mum when to jump and duck to dodge the obstacles.

But, even as a computer character, her mum wasn't very good. She got tangled in vines when Jenna had told her to duck, and had to chop her way out of them. Then she stopped to pick them up.

"Come on, Mum, this is not the time to tidy up," Jenna muttered, trying not to laugh.

The three friends found it was actually quite fun controlling their parents in the game. Knowing the adults

were actually in there doing everything the kids told them to do was quite exciting.

They quickly found out that each of the parents had different skills. Mattie and Aussie's dad was fast, and while quicksand would slow the others down, he could run across it without getting stuck. Their mum was strong and could lift boulders and logs out of their path. Jenna still hadn't worked out what her mum was good at yet, but she was sure there had to be something.

With the kids' expert moves and experience, the parents were soon blasting through the game. That was until Aussie suddenly cried, "Whoa! Watch out!" and brought his mum skidding to a halt. Jenna reacted just in time, and her mum stopped right in front of a sheer drop. Unfortunately, Mattie didn't see the drop, and his dad was running so fast, he ran right off the edge.

"Nooooo!" Mattie cried as his dad disappeared.

"Dad!" Aussie shouted.

But their dad had gone.

Chapter 8

Jenna's heart sank. What happened now? Was their dad gone for good? What happened if you died in the game?

Luckily, after just a few moments, Aussie and Mattie's dad reappeared at the top of the cliff with the others.

"Thank goodness!" Aussie sighed. But then they noticed one of the hearts at the top of the screen had disappeared. There had been three lives at the beginning. Now they only had two left.

"We have to be careful," Jenna said. "We don't want to lose any more lives if we can help it. I don't know what might happen if we lose all three, but I'd rather not find out."

The game felt a little bit less fun after that, and a lot more real. And they were still faced with the problem of getting across the valley.

"What do we do? We're stuck," Mattie said. "Do we go back?"

"No," said Jenna. "We have to keep moving forwards. There must be a way across this valley."

And then Jenna had an idea.

"The vines!" she said. "Mum picked up some vines. We might be able to use them to get across."

Sure enough, when Jenna got the vines out of her mum's bag, her mum quickly knotted them together and threw them across the gap.

"Wow! Well done, Mum!" Jenna cried, as they all made it across the vine bridge to safety.

There were plenty more challenges to face after that, but the friends worked together with their parents to make it through. Finally, they reached a door with a sign saying 'Exit'.

"That's it, we've done it! We've completed the game!" Mattie said.

"This can't really be it though, can it?" Jenna said. "It seems too easy."

"Easy?" Aussie asked. "We battled hard to get here! We've earned this!"

But Jenna wasn't so sure. The game had been tricky in parts but nowhere near as hard as she had expected it to be, especially since Graham had been so sure their parents wouldn't get out. There had to be something else,

something they were missing. But the only way onwards was through the door.

"I guess there's only one way to find out if we've done it or not," Jenna said.

The three friends led their parents up to the door. Just as Jenna's mum grabbed the door handle, a giant fell from the sky and landed on her, squashing her flat.

Another life lost.

Chapter 9

"Look! It's Graham!" Mattie cried, looking up at the giant. He dodged his dad out of the way just in time as Graham stomped around, laughing as he tried to squash the others under his huge feet.

Jenna's mum finally reappeared, and Jenna managed to get her out of the way just before Graham's giant foot landed right where she had been moments ago.

Luckily, Mattie's dad was fast, and could easily duck away from the big, slow boss. But their mum and Jenna's mum were much slower, and it was a real struggle to keep them out of harm's way.

"What are we going to do?" Aussie asked. "We can't

just keep dodging him forever."

"I don't know," Jenna said, starting to panic. This had to be the final battle. If they won this, their parents would be free. But they only had one life left, and no idea how to defeat Graham. "Every boss in a game has a weakness. We just need to find his."

"Let's work together, use our special abilities," Mattie suggested.

While Mattie made his dad dart around the room to confuse Graham, Aussie made his mum use her strength to pick Graham up and throw him across the floor, but he

always just got back up again.

But what can my mum do? Jenna thought. *She doesn't have any special ability.*

Then she remembered the rope ladder her mum had made. Maybe her ability was to make things. Jenna got the vines back out for her mum, hoping she would be able to do something with them. Immediately, her mum started making a long, twisted rope. Then she turned it into a

lasso, and expertly hooked Graham with it.

"Yes! Go, Mum!" Jenna cried as she pulled Graham crashing to the ground.

Aussie got his mum to stand on top of Graham to keep him down, and Mattie sent his dad dashing round and round him with the rest of the vine to tie him up.

"That's it! We've done it!" Mattie cried.

They waited for the game to end. Surely they had done it... they had defeated Graham. But after a few moments, Graham just broke free and stood back up again. This didn't make sense. What else could they do? How many times did they have to defeat him for them to win?

Then Jenna realised something, and her heart sank.

"He doesn't have a health bar. There's nothing we can do to stop him. We can't ever win," Jenna said sadly. "He never planned to release our parents at all!"

Chapter 10

The friends paused their game and stormed round to Graham's house.

"Let our parents go!" Jenna shouted, bursting through the front door.

"Never," Graham said calmly.

"You have to," Aussie said.

"No, actually I don't," Graham said.

"This is hopeless," Mattie sighed. "He isn't going to let them go, he never was."

But Jenna wasn't about to give up. Graham was just like a boss in a computer game. He must have a weakness somewhere, they just needed to find it.

Jenna looked around the living room. There were pictures everywhere, photos of Graham with his parents: on holiday, at the beach, camping. But Jenna noticed that they were all when Graham was younger. There weren't any recent ones.

"This looks like fun," Jenna said, pointing to a picture of Graham with his dad on rollercoaster.

Graham shrugged. "We don't do anything like that anymore. My parents are far too busy. They don't want to do anything with me. Nobody does," Graham said sadly. "But I don't need them. I don't need anyone. I've got my computer games. I'll be fine."

"But aren't you lonely?" Jenna asked.

Graham didn't respond, he just looked down at his feet.

"You know, your game was really good," Jenna said. "We would love to play with you again sometime."

"Really?" Graham asked, looking surprised. Aussie and Mattie looked just as surprised, but Jenna shot them a secret smile.

"Definitely! We love playing games with our friends," Jenna said, and Aussie and Mattie nodded, finally catching on.

"You... you'd really want to be my friend?" Graham asked.

"Yeah. You seem really smart and... fun," Aussie said.

"And I bet if you asked your parents, they would love to do more with you too," Jenna said. Graham frowned. "Just look at all these pictures, all the fun times you've had together. They love you."

"Do you really think so?"

"Of course they do. I bet they really miss you already. You don't want to be alone for the rest of your life, do you? Without any friends or family to make memories with?" Jenna asked.

Graham's bottom lip curled. And then it started to wobble. And then Graham burst into tears. Big, loud, gasping sobs.

"Whoa, what's wrong?" Aussie asked in a panic.

"I miss my mum and dad!" Graham wailed.

"It's okay," Jenna reassured him, putting her arm around him. "You can still bring them back. It's not too late," she said, hoping it was true.

Graham nodded.

"Alright," he said, blowing his nose loudly.

Jenna breathed a sigh of relief. Boss battle completed.

Chapter 11

"How did you know how to change Graham's mind like that?" Aussie asked as they rushed home.

"Every boss has a weakness," Jenna said. "As soon as I realised that he was lonely, it was easy really."

"Let's just hope it's really worked," Mattie said.

"Well, we'll soon find out," Jenna said. "See you in a bit."

Jenna ran up the path to her front door and opened it. But, as she stepped inside, her heart sank. The house was quiet. The living room was still a mess. Mum wasn't back.

Then she heard a clatter in the kitchen. Jenna rushed inside. There was her mum, doing the dishes. Jenna threw herself at her mum and gave her a huge hug.

"There you are," Mum said, hugging her back. "Sorry, love, I think I might have got a bit carried away on that computer last night. I didn't realise how much time I'd lost." She yawned and rubbed her eyes. She looked exhausted. And clearly she didn't remember everything that had happened. "I don't think I'll be playing that game again. It just took over my life!"

Jenna hid a smile. Her mum had no idea!

"You'll be pleased to know the computer is all yours again," Mum said.

Jenna gave her mum another quick hug. She was so pleased to have her back safe and sound.

"How about I give you a hand with the cleaning first?" Jenna offered, and she pulled on a pair of rubber gloves.

"What a day!" Aussie said when the friends met up online again later.

"Let's just hope our parents never try to take over our computers again. It just isn't safe for them to play computer games!" Mattie laughed. "At least we're back on now."

But suddenly Jenna didn't really feel like gaming.

"Do you know what? I think I've played enough computer games for one day. Shall we go to the park instead?" Jenna asked.

"Sounds good to us," Aussie and Mattie agreed.

"I'll meet you there in a bit, I just have to make a stop first," Jenna said.

★★★

Jenna knocked on the big front door and took a deep breath in.

The door opened, and a smiling face greeted her.

"Hi!" Graham said in surprise.

"Hi," Jenna said, smiling back. "Would you like to come to the park with me and my friends?"

Graham's face lit up, and then he sighed.

"I'm sorry. I would love to, but I'm actually just about to go out. My dad's taking me swimming." Graham gave Jenna a shy smile.

"That's great!" Jenna said enthusiastically. And she meant it. Graham seemed so much happier, and she was really pleased for him. "Maybe another time then?"

Graham grinned the biggest grin she had ever seen— Jenna was glad she had decided to give him a chance. Maybe he wasn't really a baddie after all... when he wasn't trying to capture all the grown-ups, that was!

Discussion Points

1. Who is Jenna playing video games with in the beginning?

2. What happens to Jenna's mum when she is glitched?

a) She goes on a jungle holiday

b) She is sucked into the video game

c) She stops playing on the computer

3. What was your favourite part of the story?

4. How do Jenna, Mattie and Aussie save their parents?

5. Why do you think Graham wanted to trap all the parents in the game?

6. Who was your favourite character and why?

7. There were moments in the story when Jenna had to put herself **in someone else's shoes**. Where do you think the story shows this most?

8. What do you think happens after the end of the story?

Book Bands for Guided Reading

The Institute of Education book banding system is a scale of colours that reflects the various levels of reading difficulty. The bands are assigned by taking into account the content, the language style, the layout and phonics. Word, phrase and sentence level work is also taken into consideration.

The Maverick Readers Scheme is a bright, attractive range of books covering the pink to grey bands. All of these books have been book banded for guided reading to the industry standard and edited by a leading educational consultant.

To view the whole Maverick Readers scheme, visit our website at
www.maverickearlyreaders.com

Or scan the QR code to view our scheme instantly!

Maverick Chapter Readers
(From Lime to Grey Band)